THE CASE OF THE
CURSED
CHALET

Anne Schraff

PAGETURNERS

SUSPENSE
Boneyard
The Cold, Cold Shoulder
The Girl Who Had Everything
Hamlet's Trap
Roses Red as Blood

ADVENTURE
A Horse Called Courage
Planet Doom
The Terrible Orchid Sky
Up Rattler Mountain
Who Has Seen the Beast?

MYSTERY
The Hunter
Once Upon a Crime
Whatever Happened to
  Megan Marie?
When Sleeping Dogs Awaken
Where's Dudley?

DETECTIVE
The Case of the Bad Seed
**The Case of the
  Cursed Chalet**
The Case of the Dead Duck
The Case of the Wanted Man
The Case of the Watery Grave

SCIENCE FICTION
Bugged!
Escape from Earth
Flashback
Murray's Nightmare
Under Siege

SPY
A Deadly Game
An Eye for an Eye
I Spy, e-Spy
Scavenger Hunt
Tuesday Raven

Development and Production: Laurel Associates, Inc.

SADDLEBACK
EDUCATIONAL PUBLISHING
www.sdlback.com

ISBN-13: 978-1-56254-387-7
ISBN-10: 1-56254-387-3
eBook: 978-1-60291-245-8

Printed in the United States of America

15 14 13 12 11   2 3 4 5 6 7 8 9

CONTENTS

Chapter 1

"Wait!" Nina called out. The young couple was hurrying toward their sport utility vehicle when she caught up to them. She was assistant manager at High Chalets, a ski lodge in the mountains.

"You're not leaving already?" Nina asked cheerfully. "I thought you guys were staying for a week."

This was 22-year-old Nina Blake's first job, and she was anxious to do her best. Making sure guests were happy was her number one task.

The young man shouted, "We didn't bargain for howling sounds all night! That wasn't in the brochure!"

"Not to mention those weird rapping sounds on the windows!" the young woman cried as she hurriedly threw her suitcase into the SUV parked in the driveway.

"Well, look," Nina said, "maybe somebody in the next chalet was doing too much partying. When guests have too much to drink, they can make a nuisance of themselves. But I'm sure we can straighten this out. It seems a shame for you to shorten your vacation."

But as Nina struggled to convince the guests to stay, she had a sick feeling in the pit of her stomach. These were not the first guests to be driven away from Chalet 17 because of strange, unnerving noises. Nina's boss, Mr. Cowles, had been worried about the problem for several months.

"*You* can straighten out anything you want," the man said as he slipped behind the wheel of the SUV. "All *we* want to do is get as far away from this crazy place as possible."

Nina watched the SUV roar off, then walked to the manager's apartment.

"Uh—Mr. Cowles, I'm sorry to say there was a problem in Chalet 17 again. The couple that was staying there just left in a big hurry," Nina said.

Mr. Cowles, a thin, nervous man, was pushing 50. Nina knew that he had lost his long-time job due to company downsizing. Now he was desperately trying to build a new career at this job. "What do you mean?" he demanded, his eyes wild with fear. "What happened?"

"The Osborns, the young couple in Chalet 17—they took off like bats out of hell just now. They said they heard strange noises all night and tapping sounds on the windows," Nina said.

Mr. Cowles turned pale. "What the devil!" he cried. He sat down hard in his chair and ran his hand through his thinning hair. "Chalet 17 again! More money flying out the door! Nina, do you realize we've lost five guests in less than two months? That's a lot of money down the drain! And it all affects the bottom line, you know. The owners are going to wonder why we can't get on top of this problem!"

"I tried to talk the Osborns into staying," Nina said defensively. "I'll send housekeeping down to tidy up the place for the next guests."

Mr. Cowles looked furious. "The *next* guests? Are you crazy? How long do you think this can go on? Don't be foolish, Nina. We've got a problem—a *huge* problem. And you're the one who has to get to the bottom of it! Forget all about fluffing up the pillows! Find out what's going on in Chalet 17, and put a stop to it! If you don't, both of us are history—understand?"

Nina nodded nervously. She was now just one year from her teaching credential at the state college. She wasn't a detective! What was Mr. Cowles talking about? Did he really think she was some kind of ghost buster? But Nina loved this job, and she needed the income. So she said calmly, "Well, I'll surely do my best, Mr. Cowles."

"I don't want to hear that, Nina. I want you to *solve* this problem—do you hear me? If it gets around that we have a haunted cabin here, it'll be the kiss of death for this resort. My job is on the line and so is yours!" Mr. Cowles raved.

"Okay, well—I'll get right to it and try to find out what's going on," Nina stammered, backing out of the office in Mr. Cowles' apartment.

It was a cold February morning in the high mountains. A light dusting of snow lay on the Swiss chalet-style cabins. They looked as beautiful as the pictures you see on postcards.

Nina had never dreamed she could find such a perfect job while she was still in college. It paid fairly well—and when Nina was off duty she had time to practice her favorite sport, skiing. The job also gave Nina evenings and weekends with her drop-dead cute boyfriend, ski instructor Brian Holland.

Now Nina went hunting for Brian. Like her, he was a college student who worked here to pay for his education. High Chalets was a small resort. Brian was a ski instructor when there was snow on the ground, and a janitor when there wasn't.

"Brian, got a minute?" Nina asked when she found him checking out the newly fallen snow.

"Sure," Brian said. "Darn. There's not enough snow yet for skiing. . . . "

"Brian, I told you about the spooky stuff that's been happening in Chalet 17. Well, it's happened again. A young couple went tearing out of here this morning. They seemed to be scared out of their wits. Mr. Cowles is beside himself. For some reason he expects *me* to get to the bottom of it. I don't know where to begin," Nina said.

"Could be something spooky," Brian teased. "These chalets are really old.

They were built back in the 1890s. Of course they've been remodeled and updated, but a lot of people have lived within those walls. Who knows what could have happened in Chalet 17?"

"What are you saying, Brian?" Nina asked shakily. "You think something horrible happened in that cabin? You think it's haunted or something? Some spook is marauding around at night?"

Brian shook his head. "Who knows? I've read about weird stuff like that happening. I've heard some of the guests' stories about the howling and rattling windows. . . ." he said.

"But what am I going to do? Mr. Cowles expects *me* to fix things!" Nina groaned. But then she remembered something. There was a really old house down the road from High Chalets. The place was occupied by an old man named Mr. Peebles. Nina had talked to him once. He seemed to know everyone and everything about the mountains.

"Maybe Mr. Peebles would have a clue about what happened in Chalet 17. What do you think, Brian?"

"Yeah, good idea. He knows where all the bodies are buried," Brian said.

"Don't say that, Brian!" Nina cried out with a shiver.

"Nina, come on! I just mean that he's someone who knows all the dirt. Mr. Peebles never did like this resort. Maybe he's behind the stuff that's scaring the guests. He told me once he'd like to see the mountain back like it used to be. You know—with bears and bobcats roaming around," Brian said.

"I guess I'd better talk to him," Nina said. "It's a start, anyway."

Nina climbed on her motorcycle and drove down the highway to Mr. Peebles' house. She wasn't certain he would tell her anything useful, but she didn't know where else to turn. Mr. Peebles' property adjoined the High Chalets' land. The old man's home was a frame-and-stone house that his father and grandfather had built. That was way back in a time when the land was virgin forest and a fall of fresh snow remained without footprints for weeks.

Nina got off her bike in Mr. Peebles' gravel driveway and went to the door. But then she saw Mr. Peebles walking across his yard, piling up freshly cut cordwood. "Morning, Mr. Peebles," Nina called out cheerfully.

"Hello there, young lady," Mr. Peebles said with a smile. Local people said the old man was eccentric. But he had seemed nice enough the few times Nina had talked to him. His wife had died several years ago. Nina guessed he was lonely. That must be why he kept so busy chopping wood and building birdhouses.

"Mr. Peebles, I wonder if you could help me with something. I work at High Chalets. Lately, we've been having problems in one of the cabins—Chalet

17. It seems that guests who stay there hear some kind of unearthly sounds. They get scared to death and then they leave. That's really bad for business, of course. Do you know anything about Chalet 17? Did something—uh—*unusual* happen there?" Nina asked.

Mr. Peebles nodded, his face turning serious. He sat on a downturned barrel. "That'd be the chalet on the south side, facing toward the lake? Yep, I know the one. Got a twisted pine out front, sort of like a giant wrenched it down."

"Yes, that's right," Nina said.

"It's not a fit place for people to be, young lady. I'd shut it down. Better yet, *tear* it down. Right to the ground. Plow over it. Terrible thing happened there— *terrible*. Worst thing that ever happened in these mountains. . . . " Mr. Peebles said, shaking his head from side to side.

Chapter 2

Nina felt sick. So Mr. Peebles *did* know about a horrible event that had happened at Chalet 17! But Nina wasn't *sure* that something awful had actually happened there. Maybe the old guy had dreamed it up to cause problems for the resort he hated.

A curio shop was on a small lot adjoining the Peebles property. To scare off guests, all Mr. Peebles would have to do was wander over there from time to time and spread horror stories about High Chalets.

"What are you talking about, Mr. Peebles?" Nina asked.

"Oh, the Cosgrove murder, of course. All the oldtimers around here know about that. The brothers, Amos and

Oscar—hell-raisers, they were. Especially Amos. They stood to inherit all the land from their father. 'Course Amos was greedy. He wanted it *all*. He up and murdered his own brother, don'tcha see? Killed him right there in the cabin you call Chalet 17. Now, poor Oscar's spirit is roaming around, restless as all get out," Mr. Peebles said.

"When did this happen?" Nina asked suspiciously.

"Oh, about twenty years before I was born. I was just a lad when I first heard the story. Guess that means it must've happened about a hundred years ago now," Mr. Peebles said.

"Look, Mr. Peebles, that's a *long* time ago," Nina said patiently. "I'm sure Oscar's spirit has quieted down by now. But why tell tourists about what happened in Chalet 17? Then they get scared into imagining things—and that's bad for business. Maybe it would be better if you just didn't talk about it."

Mr. Peebles' face hardened. "Folks got the *right* to know what happened! 'Specially in a place they're laying down their heads. *Bloody murder* is what happened right there. Folks are entitled to know that Oscar Cosgrove shed his life's blood right there in that cabin. I don't blame Oscar for prowling around looking for justice!" he snorted.

Nina took a long, deep breath. She doubted the story was true. Some said Mr. Peebles often made up stories—or at least embellished them so much they didn't resemble the truth anymore. Once he'd told folks that recluse-millionaire Howard Hughes had come to see him. The old man had a big imagination.

After saying goodbye, Nina went next door to the curio shop. It was run by a woman in her 60s named Amelia Menard. She had short curly gray hair and pretty blue-green eyes that sparkled behind steel-rimmed glasses.

"You've got a nice little shop here,"

Nina said as she looked around.

Amelia Menard smiled. "Well, it's really just a hole in the wall, honey. But I don't know what I'd do without it. It's my life," she said.

Nina wondered if Amelia would know about the Cosgrove murder. Perhaps she'd have a more truthful slant. "You know, I've been talking to Mr. Peebles. He told me about a murder that supposedly happened around here a hundred years ago," Nina said.

Amelia Menard smiled. "Well, Leo Peebles *says* it was murder—but the sheriff said it was an accident. Seems that two brothers were playing around, wrestling. One of them got a broken neck. Freak accident. It was sad, though. I've seen stories in old newspapers. Nice-looking boys, they were. But Leo is pretty sure it was murder, and Leo is a solid man. The salt of the earth. Still, when he gets a notion, he's stubborn. He won't let go of it any more than a hungry bulldog will cut loose a bone."

Nina was relieved to hear a more rational story. She explained what had recently been happening in Chalet 17. "My boss is really upset, Ms. Menard. We've lost a number of guests over this nonsense. I just wish Mr. Peebles wouldn't be feeding people's fear with his wild stories," Nina said.

"My goodness!" Amelia Menard said. "Well, I'll tell Leo to go easy on the ghost stories. It probably won't do any good, though. He thinks that justice wasn't done because Amos Cosgrove was never hung for killing his brother."

"Why? You can't hang someone for an *accident*," Nina said.

"That's for sure," the woman said with a pleasant smile. Nina liked her. Mrs. Menard was like a breath of fresh air after the cranky Mr. Peebles.

Nina felt a little better as she climbed on her motorcycle for the short ride back to the resort. Maybe she'd made some headway in solving the problem. If only Ms. Menard could get Mr. Peebles to stop talking about the murder and the avenging ghost!

Nina smiled as the cool breeze ruffled the bangs on her forehead. "Wow," she thought, "I've been a detective for just a few hours—and already I'm solving the case!" The problem was Mr. Peebles. His wild tales were stirring up the incoming guests. That's why they imagined scary things in Chalet 17.

Later that afternoon, Nina and Brian enjoyed some hot cider in the lobby of the High Chalets lodge. The weatherman on TV was promising a heavy spring snow. Both Nina and Brian hoped for white-clad hills and some great skiing.

"I talked to Mr. Peebles, Brian. It seems that the old guy is spooking people with horror stories. I talked to his neighbor—a real nice lady—and she promised to get him to stop scaring people off if she could," Nina said.

"Actually, Mr. Peebles really does think there was a murder in Chalet 17. He said it happened about a hundred years ago. That's what he's been building on."

"A *murder* actually happened in the cabin?" Brian asked curiously.

"Probably it was just an accident. Two brothers were fighting, and one got his neck broken," Nina said.

"Wow," Brian said.

"People are so gullible," Nina said. "After hearing this bizarre story, the guests imagine all sorts of frightening stuff once they get in the cabin."

When they finished their cider, Nina made the rounds of the chalets. She was trying to be especially accommodating to the guests. If word of her extra efforts got back to Mr. Cowles, it might help.

When Nina got to Chalet 17, it was still empty, just as the Osborns had left it. Nina went in and looked around. Inside, the chalets were all alike. They all had Swiss-style architecture, a high loft, and a big stone fireplace and hearth.

An idea came to her. The more she thought about it, the more she liked it. She lived in a room at the lodge as the other employees did. But what was to stop her from spending the night in Chalet 17? That would give her solid proof that nothing weird was going on there! Then she would know *for sure* that the guests had already been frightened before they got there.

Nina had no doubt that any noises could be easily explained. A pine tree branch scratching on the window. The wind rattling the rafters. The distant cry of a wolf, or maybe even a stray dog!

"Yeah," Nina thought to herself, "that's what I'll do—check the place out for myself!"

It would be sort of fun living in the luxurious chalet, sleeping in one of those marvelous beds. The bed in her room in the lodge was lumpy, and the decor was Spartan. The owners of High

Chalets weren't about to provide elegant quarters for their lowly employees.

First, Nina checked out the area around the chalet. Then she went inside carrying her small overnight bag. It contained only her pajamas, makeup, soaps, and a few other personal items.

She settled into the recliner with the built-in massager. Before now, she had only sat in these recliners at department stores. "Cool," she said. "So this is how the rich folks live!" Nina figured that a recliner like this cost about as much as she earned in two months!

Looking outdoors, she noticed that it was dark now. Large, blurry snowflakes were falling. Nina hoped there would be a good solid snow pack by tomorrow.

Then, just outside the window, Nina thought she heard the muffled sobs of a human voice. She sat up quickly, almost tumbling from the recliner. Her legs seemed to have gone numb. For a minute she just sat there, frozen.

Chapter 3

"Hey, this is stupid!" Nina cried aloud. She grabbed her fleece-lined jacket and put it on. Surely she was overreacting. Some guest walking by was probably having a fight with her husband. Now she was bawling in the darkness—that was all.

Nina thought about how quickly imagination can kick in. You hear a perfectly normal sound, and right away it sounds like the ghostly moans of Oscar Cosgrove!

Nina opened the chalet door and called out, "Who's there?"

Moving out from the cabin, Nina cast the beam of her flashlight around. Everything looked eerie and unreal in the moonlight, but she couldn't see anyone. Was the sound she'd heard really crying? Or was it just the wind?

"Who's out there?" Nina shouted. "Hellooo. Do you need any help? I'm the assistant manager, and if you're having a problem. . . " Nina's voice trailed away when her flashlight beam shone on something awful. It was a bloody rag tied around a whisky bottle! It lay in the snow, about ten feet from the back door of the chalet.

"Anybody out here?" Nina shouted in a shaky voice. She took a closer look at the bloody whisky bottle. Maybe that wasn't blood at all, she thought. Maybe her imagination was working overtime.

Nina went to see Mr. Cowles. She had to show him what she had found. As the boss, Mr. Cowles and his wife lived in a fairly nice apartment in the lodge. But it was nothing like the rooms provided for the paying guests.

"Oh, it's you. What is it, Nina?" Mr. Cowles frowned as he opened the door.

"Is there another problem?"

"I want to show you something outside Chalet 17," Nina said.

When he saw the whisky bottle, Mr. Cowles quickly turned away. "Get rid of it," he shouted, as if he had had enough. *"Just get rid of it.* It's got to be some sick fool's idea of a joke! I'm telling you, there are people out to *ruin* this place! You have to find out who they are!"

Nina decided not to say a word about the crying sounds. Mr. Cowles already seemed to be getting hysterical. Instead, she thought hard as she walked back to the lodge with her boss.

"Mr. Cowles, do you know anything about the Cosgrove family?" she asked. "You know—the people who used to own this land?"

"The Cosgrove family?" he muttered. "No, I never heard—wait, yes, I know! There's a portrait of some wretched old man in the living room of the lodge. It's by the fireplace. He has weird, piercing eyes that seem to follow you around the room. Mrs. Chance told me the old man was her great-grandfather. That's right— his name was Cosgrove."

Mrs. Chance? She was the owner of the lodge. Nina had never spoken to her, but she had seen the older woman driving up in her Lincoln Continental.

"I've seen Mrs. Chance," Nina said.

"She's a witch," Mr. Cowles said heatedly. "A harder woman I've never met. She just loves to fire people! The old girl absolutely feeds on power. If the bottom line here at the lodge doesn't show an upturn pretty soon, she'll have my scalp for sure!"

As they passed through the lodge, Nina glanced up at the portrait of old Mr. Cosgrove. Suddenly, a chill went up her spine. His deep-set black eyes really *did* seem to follow her as she moved across the room!

Chapter 4

Nina wondered if the man in the portrait was the father of the boys, Oscar and Amos. Or was he one of them? He might be Amos Cosgrove in his old age.

"I must go to bed now," Mr. Cowles said. "I need to take my sedatives. I take pills to calm my nerves, pills to put me to sleep, pills to ease my stomach problems and headaches—oh, what headaches I get! It's all nerves, you know." His eyes looked frantic as he turned toward Nina.

"I'm almost fifty. I don't get many more chances to start over in life. I can't afford to lose another job. My wife told me that if I lose another job, she's had it. She's talking about filing for divorce. Do you see what I'm up against? You've *got* to help me, Nina, or I'm done for. We *must* find out who's trying to ruin this resort, and stop them!"

"I'll work really hard on it," Nina promised. She felt sorry for Mr. Cowles. He was clearly losing it. She had heard that he was deeply in debt. As a young man he'd married a beautiful society girl. She'd expected that he'd be at the top of his game by now. At one time he'd been in line to be CEO at a Fortune 500 company. Now he was trying to save an old resort hotel. He seemed to think it was his last chance to make good. Maybe it was.

After Mr. Cowles left, Nina was alone in the big living room of the lodge. She walked closer to the portrait of the stern old man so she could study it. He had tendrils of white hair sprouting from his nostrils and ears, as well as shaggy sideburns tapering down into a pointed beard. His mean-looking mouth was a grim line. Nina read the faded name at the bottom of the old painting:

Amos Waldo Cosgrove

Nina stood there, staring at the picture of the long-dead man. So he *had* been one of the boys who took part in that deadly struggle 100 years ago! He was the one who killed his brother, the one who had lived—and inherited the family fortune. Then suddenly, a very weird, creepy feeling came over Nina. She felt like she was peering into an ancient tomb and discovering the mummified remains of a tyrant!

Nina glanced around the room, looking at other portraits that she had never noticed before. There was a pudgy man named Waldo Cosgrove, the old man's son. He'd been dead a long time, too. Then there was a skinny man with glasses named Waldo Jr. Finally, there was a picture of an arrogant-looking woman who was probably not as beautiful as her painted portrait. Her name was Deidre "Dee-Dee" Chance.

She was the great-great-granddaughter of old Amos Waldo Cosgrove.

Mrs. Chance.

The old man and his offspring had done well, Nina thought. Luckily for them, they hadn't had to share the family money way back when the one brother died—by intent or accident. Now everything belonged to the progeny of Amos Cosgrove, the brother who had survived the battle in Chalet 17.

Nina returned to the chalet. She found some kitchen tongs and carefully picked up the whisky bottle with the bloody rag around it. Then she dropped the whole thing in a bucket and hid it in one of the storage sheds. She didn't want to destroy it. Who knew what might come up later on? Perhaps it would be needed as evidence of vandalism.

"Well, here goes nothing," Nina muttered to herself as she went inside Chalet 17 again. She closed and locked the door. As she had planned, she was determined to spend the rest of the night here. Now, though, it wasn't the fun adventure she had thought it would be. She didn't feel like luxuriating in the expensive massage recliner or enjoying the fantastic bed. Now there was a fearful edge to being here. *She had heard someone sobbing.* At least she thought she had. And then there was the bottle and the bloody rag.

As she got ready for bed, Nina kept thinking about the muffled sobs. She didn't seriously think it was the troubled ghost of young Oscar Cosgrove—but it did seem that there was something evil around here.

Nina didn't put on her pajamas right away. But she didn't feel like crawling into bed, either. So after she brushed her teeth and showered, she dressed in her jogging clothes and went back to the recliner. She covered herself up with a comforter and turned on the radio.

About midnight something startled her. Nina's eyes snapped open and she was instantly wide awake. Was there someone at the window? *Yes!* She heard another tapping sound. Nina got out of the recliner as soundlessly as she could. She wanted to creep out the front door and take a look around the corner. Maybe a bird or a windblown branch was making the noise at the back window.

But when Nina went out and looked around the corner, what she saw was a shadowy human figure. It was running from the back of the chalet toward the deep, dark woods.

Cold perspiration popped out all over Nina's shivering body.

Chapter 5

The figure quickly disappeared into the first dark row of snowy trees. Not enough snow had fallen to make the tracks visible, but now Nina knew for sure that *somebody* was harassing the guests in Chalet 17. She had not gotten a good enough look at the figure to see if it was a man or a woman. She did notice, however, that the figure was clad in a long, dark cloak.

Could it have been Mr. Peebles? He was 80, but he was remarkably spry. Nina had seen him scrambling up ladders to trim trees. He could have sprinted off as quickly as the figure did.

Maybe it *was* Mr. Peebles, Nina thought. After all, he was very angry about the unpunished death of Oscar

Cosgrove! Maybe he'd taken it upon himself to wreak vengeance on the murderer's descendants. The old man seemed eccentric enough for anything.

Or maybe it was the ghost of Oscar Cosgrove. Nina had never really believed in such things—but she knew that unexplained things *did* happen.

Searching for clues, Nina continued to walk around the outside of the cabin for a while. Suddenly, she heard the crackle of a twig. She turned sharply to see a figure emerge from the woods. Even though she was usually fairly brave, Nina had no desire to confront the intruder. Mr. Cowles wanted her to solve this case—but Nina Blake was just a college student, not a detective. She was hurrying back toward the cabin when she glimpsed the figure again. This time she recognized who it was.

"Mr. Cowles!" Nina gasped. "What are you doing out here, sneaking around in the dark?"

Mr. Cowles' long, dark overcoat was speckled with snow. "I couldn't sleep!" he said. "I thought I'd come down here and have a look around for myself. What about *you*, young lady? Why are you wandering around in the dark?"

"I heard tapping at the window," Nina said. She stared at Mr. Cowles. For the first time, she had doubts about her boss. Had *he* been tapping on the window? Could he have some hidden motive for upsetting the hotel guests? Maybe his whole tale of woe was a lie. How could she be sure? It could be that Mr. Cowles *wasn't* working in the best interests of Mrs. Chance.

"Tapping at the window? Are you sure?" Mr. Cowles asked.

"It sure sounded like it," Nina said.

Mr. Cowles glanced at the place where the bloody rag wrapped around the whisky bottle had been. "You got rid of that monstrous thing, didn't you? I was afraid you'd leave it until morning and a guest might find it," he said.

"I took care of it," Nina said. "Mr. Cowles, excuse me for saying this, but you seem—uh—strange."

"*Strange?* What are you talking about?" Mr. Cowles growled. He seemed a little unsteady on his feet, and Nina wondered if he had been drinking.

"You seem—uh—like you might be ill," Nina said diplomatically. "Have you been drinking?"

"How dare you say such a thing!" Mr. Cowles snapped. "A kid like you! Have you no respect for your employer? I hired you, and I can fire you. I don't need some little twit commenting on my private life. So I took a couple of drinks to calm myself down—so what? I assure you that I'm perfectly all right."

"I'm sorry, Mr. Cowles," Nina said, imagining her job flying south like a flock of geese. "I'm really sorry."

"Well, you *should* be," Mr. Cowles grumbled. He made a show of carefully brushing the snow off the shoulders of his coat. Then he walked—carefully but unsteadily—back toward the lodge. Soon he was out of sight.

Nina's imagination ran wild. She couldn't help suspecting that something *peculiar* was going on with Mr. Cowles. But what could it be? She didn't have a clue.

Chapter 6

Late the next morning, Nina met Brian for waffles and coffee in the employees' lounge. She told him about last night's strange events.

"Mr. Cowles gives me the creeps," Brian said. "He's always so jumpy and nervous—like he's hiding something. If this wasn't such a perfect job for me, I wouldn't work for that bozo for two days." Then Brian laughed. "But where else can I get paid for being a ski bum?"

Nina looked worried. "But Brian, think about it. Why would Mr. Cowles want to be creeping around and tapping on the window to scare me? He knew I was in that cabin," Nina said. "He claims he wanted to make sure I'd gotten rid of that bloody rag—"

Brian's mouth fell open. "Nina! *What* bloody rag?" he asked in a shocked voice.

"Oh, I guess I forgot to tell you that. I found this bloody rag wrapped around a whisky bottle on the ground by Chalet 17. You know—like somebody was trying to send me some kind of threatening message. Of course I'm not absolutely sure it was real blood—but it sure looked like it," Nina said.

Brian frowned. "You should get it checked out," he said.

"Oh, sure. Can't you just see what would happen? We'd have police crawling all around the place, scaring even more guests away," Nina sighed.

Brian looked at his watch. "Oh, it's almost time! I gotta go bring Amelia her burger and fries," he said.

"Are you talking about Amelia Menard? You're bringing her burgers and fries?" Nina asked in surprise.

"Sure," Brian laughed. "She's a neat

lady, and I really like her. We haven't had much snow this year, and it's really cut down on trade at her curio shop. So sometimes I go down there and bring her lunch. If I don't, Amelia doesn't eat anything but peanut butter and jelly sandwiches for lunch and dinner."

"That's real nice of you, Brian," Nina said. "She seems like a nice lady. She promised to help us stop Mr. Peebles from spreading ghost stories about the resort. Hey, Brian, why don't I ride down there with you? You can use my motorcycle, and I'll ride on the back."

Brian laughed. "Let's take my pickup. We got a pretty big wind chill factor going this morning," he said.

In 15 minutes they were just outside the curio shop.

"Oh, Brian, aren't you the thoughtful guy," Amelia said with a grin. She looked at Nina and smiled. "If I were a little bit younger, my dear, I'd try to steal this nice boy away from you!"

For a while, Nina and Brian made small talk with the friendly shop owner. Then Nina brought up the Cosgrove murder. "I was wondering if Oscar Cosgrove is buried around here," she asked.

"Oh, yes, dear. All the Cosgroves are buried in the cemetery at Alpine Ridge. They have a family plot there. Why? Do you want to see his grave?" Amelia asked.

Before Nina could answer, Mr. Peebles came walking into the store. Nina could tell that he'd overheard the last part of their conversation. "Whose grave?" he demanded.

"Hello there, Leo. We were talking about Oscar Cosgrove's grave," Amelia answered.

Mr. Peebles laughed sharply. "Oh, he's not there. No, sir. Oscar Cosgrove is out and about these days, dontcha know? And he's going to be making it good and hot for everybody until he gets some justice!" the old man cackled.

"Come on!" Nina laughed. "How do you get justice for a man who's been dead for a hundred years? You say that his brother killed him—but his brother is dead, too. So what's the point?"

Mr. Peebles glared at Nina, a cold gleam of fury in his eyes. "You don't get it, girlie. You don't get it at all. When Amos Waldo Cosgrove murdered his brother, he got the whole inheritance. There was *blood* on that money, dontcha see? The least Oscar deserves is that the truth be told. We owe him that, plain and simple," he said stubbornly.

Chapter 7

Nina and Brian climbed back in Brian's old pickup truck. Nina sighed. "Why does Mr. Peebles care so much? I can't understand it, Brian. That old crime—if it *was* a crime—has nothing to do with him. Yet he's so angry, I wouldn't be surprised if *he's* the one who's causing trouble at Chalet 17."

Brian nodded. "I hear you. He *does* seem to be more than just an old guy with a passion for justice."

Then Nina had an idea. "Brian, could you spare the time to take me down to Alpine Ridge?" she asked.

"You want to see the grave, huh?" Brian asked. "What do you think you'll find, madame detective—an empty spot where the guy crawled out?" There was a wry grin on Brian's face. Nina saw that he was trying to lighten things up.

Nina laughed. "Okay, Brian—humor me. I just want to see the marker and whatever else is there," she said.

They drove for about 30 minutes, and as the elevation dropped, the weather became warmer. It never snowed at the 2,500-foot level where small hills were dotted with scrub brush.

Little Alpine Ridge had remained unchanged over the years. It was easy to find the Founders Cemetery, as it was called. Brian rode through the open iron gates. And just as he did, a man who had been working on the sprinkler system walked toward them.

"It's Mr. Peebles!" Brian gasped. "How did he get down here so fast? We were just talking to him up at the store. I didn't see him pass us on the road."

But as the tall, lanky man drew closer, they saw that he was not Mr. Peebles. But the old man looked enough like Mr. Peebles to be his brother.

"Hello, there!" Brian called out. "You look a lot like Mr. Leo Peebles, the fella who lives up the mountain."

The man grinned over missing teeth. "Sure do. No mistake about that. I'm Gus Peebles, Leo's kid brother. I'm only eighty-one, and that old geezer is eighty-three!" Then he laughed with a raspy, crackling sound like that of dry leaves being crushed underfoot. "I'm the groundskeeper here. Sometimes I'm the gravedigger, too. I've been doing this job since I was about seventeen. Before that, my daddy did the honors. You kids looking for anybody in particular?"

"Yes," Nina said, "Oscar Cosgrove."

The pleasant expression on the old man's face faded away. "Oh, yeah," he said, "you mean the fellow who got murdered by his brother."

"Some people say so," Nina said.

"So, are you two kin or something?" Gus Peebles asked as he led Nina and

Brian on a long walk up a grassy knoll.

"No," Nina said. "I'm just looking into some strange stuff that's been going on at High Chalets. You know, the ski resort just up the road. We work there. Lately, there's been some wild talk about ghosts—"

"Well, seems to me that kind of talk isn't so wild," Gus Peebles said. "The dead don't rest when they ain't been avenged, you know. Well, here we are. That's the Cosgrove plot right there. It's behind those white block walls—the nicest plot in the cemetery. The parents are buried there along with the brothers, side by side."

Gus Peebles chuckled in a harsh way. "That's not saying they went to the same place in the afterlife, dontcha know. Mighty glad *I* wasn't old Amos when he took leave of this world. I'd have been shaking in my boots about the judgment coming for what I'd done."

Brian and Nina followed the old man

into the walled family plot. The gravestones were large upright chunks of marble. There were little bronze vases at the heads of the various graves, but none of them contained flowers. "Wintertime now," Gus explained. "No flowers around. Folks *could* bring silk flowers, I suppose—if anybody cared. Truth is, nobody comes here much anymore." The old man frowned. "It ain't right. I say them that forget the dead don't deserve to live—but that's just my opinion. My daddy used to tell me that not a soul ever came to Oscar's grave—except for the woman, of course. She'd come and bring wildflowers that she'd picked in the fields—"

Nina looked at him sharply. "What woman?" she asked.

"Oh, Oscar had a girlfriend. It was all hush-hush 'cause she came from the wrong side of the tracks. A bad match, see—a rich boy and a poor, raggedy girl. But after he was murdered, she was the only one who came to remember him. She was faithful, too. My daddy seen her month after month, year after year. Then I'd see her. 'Course by then she wasn't young no more. She was worn and tired. Then she died. After that, nobody came. The brother never came at all. I guess that's no surprise, though." A wry smile curled Gus's lips.

"Mr. Peebles," Nina said, "this stuff about Amos killing Oscar—I don't get it. Why would the parents stand for that? I just don't understand how parents would cover up for one son in the murder of the other."

Gus Peebles nodded. "People are strange, girlie. Sometimes the mind just won't *let* you believe what's plain as day to everybody else. We end up believing that we got to believe.

"Look at what those folks had to deal with. They had two sons. One was dead. No way of changing that. You think they wanted to see the other son—their last child—hanged for committing murder?

"So they made themselves believe it was just an accident. And I expect they didn't want to spend too much time thinking about it. So they never came to see the dead boy's grave. Seems to me they kinda pretended he never was . . ." His voice trailed off.

Nina knelt down at the big granite marker over Oscar Cosgrove's grave. She read the inscription aloud:

Oscar Raymond Cosgrove
Beloved son and brother

Gus Peebles stood there, laughing bitterly. "Ha! He wasn't beloved by his brother, that's for sure. That's a lie in stone, is what it is," he said.

Nina looked up. "Do you remember the name of the woman who used to visit the grave?" she asked.

"No. Just a gal in a blue shawl. She always brought wildflowers. Especially violets. Sometimes in the winter she'd bring a decorated pine cone," Gus said.

"Well, Mr. Peebles, thanks a lot for your time," Nina said to the old man. "We really appreciate your help."

"You say hi to Leo for me. I don't get up the mountain too often, and he don't get down. I'm real sorry I can't recall the gal's name for you, miss. . . I knew it once, but things slip my mind lately," Gus Peebles said as Nina and Brian waved goodbye.

Then, just as Brian started the engine, the old man came running. "*Annabel!*" he shouted. "I remember now. It was the name from that poem that Edgar Allan Poe wrote. *Annabel Lee*. Yes, sir. I always connected the poem to her 'cause it was a sad poem—and she always seemed sad. Her name was Annabel Sturm. The lady in the blue shawl. Annabel Sturm."

"Thanks a lot, Mr. Peebles," Nina said, waving to him as they drove off. As they headed up the mountain, Nina said, "It must have been really sad for her, losing a boyfriend like that."

"I suppose the Cosgroves shunned her," Brian said. "Rich people like that wouldn't want anything to do with a poor girl. Especially back then. Why, they probably hated her guts."

As the pickup drew closer to the resort, Brian turned toward Nina. "You're not spending another night in Chalet 17, are you?" he asked.

"I have to," Nina said. "It's my job to find out what's going on."

"Nina, it might be dangerous! Maybe the person causing the problem is violent. You could get hurt if you got in his way. Look, I have to go down to the airport tonight to pick up some guests. I won't be back until morning.

"Promise me you won't go near the chalet tonight. Then tomorrow night we can both hang out there and try to get to the bottom of this thing," Brian said.

"Okay," Nina agreed—but she wasn't sure she would keep her promise. She wasn't really afraid of Mr. Peebles. And she certainly wasn't buying all that nonsense about Oscar Cosgrove's ghost. She was a grown woman. She couldn't be scared off her job by silly shenanigans like tapping on windows and smearing fake blood on an old rag.

Anyway—if even one more guest got scared out of Chalet 17, Nina figured it was the end of her job at the resort. By now, word had to be getting around that the High Chalets resort was haunted. What would happen when old Mrs. Chance realized that the bottom line was getting worse instead of better? The old lady would probably raze the whole place and sell off the land.

That night was cold and miserable. There were snow flurries and a biting wind. But Nina put on her heavy thermal clothing and decided to hang out near Chalet 17 for a while. She wanted to observe what was going on. Before she went out, she filled a Thermos with coffee to help her keep warm.

Mr. Cowles had said that guests would soon be checking into Chalet 17. So tonight might be Nina's last chance to nail the culprit. If Mr. Peebles came creeping out of the woods and began howling and rapping on the windows, Nina would be ready to call the police. She liked the old man. But he couldn't be allowed to ruin somebody's business because of a 100-year-old crime!

In spite of the hot coffee, Nina was freezing. Hiding in a clump of trees, she did jumping jacks to warm up. She hoped Mr. Peebles wouldn't take too long to get here. With any luck, this whole thing could be wrapped up early.

Nina was on her third cup of coffee when she saw the dark outline of a man creeping out of the woods. She snapped to attention, fighting off the shivers in her arms and legs.

Nina's heart was pounding hard. But she kept telling herself it was only Mr. Peebles, coming to play his silly games.

Then suddenly, she couldn't see the figure anymore. Had he gone back into the woods? Nina brushed snowflakes from her eyebrows and looked around.

Where was the dark figure she had seen just a minute ago? Surely he couldn't have vanished into thin air!

Unless he was a ghost. . .

"Stop it! Don't be ridiculous," Nina scolded herself.

Then she saw the figure again. This time it was right behind her, standing between her and the cabin.

It wasn't Mr. Peebles.

Chapter 8

The man behind Nina was tall and well-built. His head and shoulders were covered with snowflakes. His long, stringy hair looked like it had once been jet black. But now it was a grayish color—although he appeared to be only in his late 30s. He was a handsome man, dressed in a long, black overcoat—the kind that was rarely seen on the street anymore. With a long black scarf wrapped around his neck, he looked like a man from a long past era.

Nina wanted to run—but the man was too close to her. She'd never be able to run fast enough to get away.

"Who are you?" she yelled into the wind, trying to sound calm.

"My name is Oscar," the man said in

a faltering voice. There was something strange and frightening about him.

"*Oscar?*" Nina repeated. "Well, can I help you? I work here. It's pretty cold out tonight. Too cold to be standing around outside—don't you think?"

"I *had* to come here," the man said in a deep baritone voice. "This is where it happened."

Nina's knees were growing weak. "No way," she said to herself. "I *can't* be talking to a ghost." This kind of thing just didn't happen—at least to her. This could *not* be Oscar Raymond Cosgrove standing before her. She had seen his grave. That man had died 100 years ago!

Nina pulled herself together. "Do you live around here?" she asked him.

The man took a step closer to Nina. "I *used* to live here. This was my home. All around here," he said.

"Well, you'd better go back to wherever you live now," Nina said. "It's getting colder. The weatherman said it might drop below freezing tonight."

"Do you know about the murder that took place in this cabin?" the man asked.

"Well, yes—I've heard stories," Nina said in a shaky voice.

"They aren't just *stories,* miss. That murder really happened. And a vile, cowardly killing it was. Done for the money, you know. Of course everyone tried to say it was just a case of two brothers scuffling—but that's not what happened.

"Amos Cosgrove wanted all the inheritance for himself. Oh, yes, it was murder all right," he said. "Everybody was on his side, though. Even the law. All of them covered it up." He fell silent for a moment and squinted at Nina. "*You* probably were in on it, too. You helped cover it up. . . . "

"No, no," Nina said, growing more and more frightened as he stepped closer. "I wasn't even born when it happened!"

"You're probably lying. Everybody lied and covered up. *Everybody*. They thought they could get away with it forever. But murder will eventually come out, you know. Sooner or later, the blood of the dead rises up to accuse the guilty." Then he sighed and turned slowly, like a man in a dream. Without another word, the tall, snow-speckled man began walking away toward the woods.

Nina thought she was going to faint. She grabbed onto a tree branch to steady herself. Then she turned and ran as fast as she could back into Chalet 17.

Chapter 9

Nina sat down until she stopped shaking. The guy she'd been talking to was a real person, not a spirit. The man was obviously disturbed. Somehow he'd heard about the old murder and then built a fantasy around it. Maybe the poor guy actually thought he *was* Oscar Raymond Cosgrove, but that was clearly impossible. . . .

When she'd calmed down, Nina went to Mr. Cowles' office. As she told him what had just happened, he listened intently, seeming pleased. "Well, then, that's it. There must be a crazy hermit living in the woods who wanders in to howl and carry on. In the morning I'll call the police. They'll roust him from whatever cave he's hiding in—and that will be the end of it! You've done a good job, Nina."

"What will he be arrested for?" Nina asked. "He didn't really do anything worse than a little mischief."

"Trespassing!" Mr. Cowles snapped. "He trespassed on our property. Right now—if he's holed up in some nearby cave—he's *still* trespassing. Mrs. Chance owns everything for miles around. It's all her property. The only land she doesn't own is the parcel old Mr. Peebles is sitting on—and that ramshackle curio shop next door.

"But Mrs. Chance hired some lawyers last year. It didn't take them long to find a defect in the deeds to those properties. You'll see, Nina. Before very much longer, Peebles and the Menard woman are going to be evicted."

"Really?" Nina gasped in surprise. "But that seems so cruel!"

"Nonsense!" Mr. Cowles grumbled. "The resort needs room to expand.

Peebles' house and the curio shop are eyesores. Those old people have to move on—move into a resthome where people of their age belong." Mr. Cowles seemed in high spirits now that his problems with Chalet 17 seemed to be solved.

The next morning a middle-aged couple moved into Chalet 17. Mr. Cowles already had the sheriff out searching for the intruder Nina had described. He was confident that no more unhappy events would cause problems at Chalet 17.

Nina and Brian went down to see Ms. Menard in her curio shop.

"I'm really sorry you're losing this place. Mr. Cowles told me the resort is taking over your property," Nina said.

Amelia Menard smiled sadly. "Well, into each life some rain must fall. My father always said that. But then—who knows the future?"

Nina told Ms. Menard about the man she had seen last night, claiming to be

Oscar Cosgrove. "It was so weird. I almost believed him," Nina said.

"Oh, the man you're talking about *is* Oscar Cosgrove," Amelia Menard said.

"That's impossible. Oscar Cosgrove has been dead for a hundred years!" Nina cried.

"Oh, yes, the one who was *murdered* is dead—but the man you met is his great-great-grandson. When Oscar died, he left a son," Ms. Menard said. "Oscar died before the boy was born. The mother, Annabel Sturm, moved to another town. But she often took the bus in to visit Oscar's grave. She raised her son in poverty. Then that son married, and there were more offspring. The boy you met—he's had his problems."

"Wow," Nina said, "then that whole side of the family was cheated out of its inheritance! Oscar's children were poor and Amos's were rich. In a way, I can't blame them. It doesn't seem right."

Ms. Menard nodded. "It was a

ghastly injustice. Just pondering it has unhinged the mind of this young man. But there was never a thing anyone could do about it. You see, the Cosgrove family simply refused to believe that Oscar was the father of Annabel Sturm's child," she said.

Nina felt sick. The mysterious picture was becoming much clearer now. Amos Cosgrove killed his brother. Then, adding insult to injury, Amos and all his dependents enjoyed luxury—while the offspring of the murdered Oscar got nothing!

Nina figured the grandson *had* to be the guy who'd been harassing High Chalets! Of course! He felt his ancestor and all his family had been wronged.

But soon the whole sad story would come to an end. When the sheriff found him, the young man would surely be whisked off to jail or to a hospital. And that would be the final triumph of the bloody deed of 100 years ago.

Chapter 10

The next morning a black Lincoln Continental drove up the mountain road to the resort. Then Mr. Cowles called Nina into his office, and she met Deidre Chance for the first time. After what Nina had heard about the woman, she expected not to like her much. But when Nina was face to face with Mrs. Chance, she liked her even less. Everything about the woman seemed cold, calculating, and absolutely heartless.

Dee Dee Chance went on and on about her plans to expand the resort. "Those ridiculous old people down the mountain have stood in our way for too long. They've been holding almost 100 acres of our valuable land—hemming us in and preventing expansion! But our lawyers found a small error in their title to the land. As I say, a *small* error—but sufficient to get rid of them and go full speed ahead with our plans."

"Excellent, wonderful!" Mr. Cowles said. He was fawning over the spoiled woman so much that it made Nina sick. "You're a *marvelous* business woman, Mrs. Chance. I'm sure your illustrious ancestor would be proud of you today."

Mrs. Chance finally turned to Nina. "I understand you're the clever little lady who uncovered who was harassing Chalet 17. Some dirty mountain man, I understand. It's unfortunate, isn't it? Reputable people shouldn't have to put up with such complications in their lives! But I'm sure the sheriff will soon find him and drag him off."

Nina felt disgusted. She was unwisely tempted to insult Mrs. Chance, but something else intervened. The middle-aged couple who had just taken Chalet 17 came rushing into the office.

They were clearly in a state of hysteria.

"It's an *outrage*!" the man gasped. "A hideous bloody object came flying through our window and landed on the bed! Lydia and I were just sitting down to coffee, and here comes a bloody cow's skull crashing through the glass! I'm warning you people—we intend to sue for the stress this has caused us!"

"What?" Mr. Cowles gasped. "I can't believe this. The sheriff promised to take care of this madman!"

"I tell you it was a disgusting cow skull, covered with blood—or something that looked like blood," the man went on. "Oh, it was the most awful thing we've ever seen! We're leaving right now, but you'll hear from our lawyer!"

The woman was clutching her head. "You people have no right to rent a cabin where such horrible things happen!" she said in a trembling voice.

When the couple went stamping out, Mrs. Chance turned a cold face to Mr.

Cowles. "I thought you just said this problem had been solved. You *idiot*! It seems that it's worse than ever!" she cried in a shrill voice.

"Please, Mrs. Chance," Nina's boss stammered, "I honestly believed that it would be taken care of by now. I cannot understand how such a thing—"

Just then the phone rang. Mr. Cowles picked it up and listened. At first he looked relieved, but then shocked. When he put down the phone, he said, "This Oscar Cosgrove . . . he's been questioned by the police . . . but they found him in *Chicago*! It seems that he took a flight to the Midwest last night."

"That's impossible!" Mrs. Chance screamed, pounding her fist on the desk. "You pack of fools! You told me that a crazy mountain man has been doing all the harassing. Cowles, I'll see that you never get another job—once I fire you here! You are incompetent! Do you hear me, absolutely *incompetent!*"

Nina slipped from the room and stopped briefly in Chalet 17. It was just as the angry couple had said. There was a sun-bleached cow's skull on the bed, dripping red liquid. Looking closer she could see that it wasn't really blood, but it surely looked like it. The floor was littered with broken glass.

Nina drove her motorcycle down to the curio shop. She went inside to find Ms. Menard rearranging her ceramic souvenirs. There were many little figures of cowboys, Native Americans, horses, and cattle. There was also a display of several cow skulls, horseshoes, and other western mementoes.

"Ms. Menard, the sheriff just called, and I thought you should know. He told me that this guy you said was Oscar Cosgrove's great-great-grandson . . . he's in Chicago," Nina said.

Ms. Menard smiled and said, "I know, dear. I told him to get out of here. I warned him that they'd blame him for everything. So I gave him the money for a ticket, and he left late last night."

"Ms. Menard, is he your son?" Nina asked softly. For the first time, she had noticed the similarity between her eyes and the eyes of the young man.

"Why, yes," Ms. Menard admitted. "He's always had problems—but he's a fine young man. He would never harm anyone or even damage property."

"But *somebody* has been doing some pretty awful vandalism at High Chalets, Ms. Menard," Nina said. "Just this morning a cow skull was hurled through the window of the cabin!"

Ms. Menard's smile deepened. "Yes. And my son was in Chicago."

"Then—" Nina said, staring at the slim, athletic woman before her. Ms. Menard was only about five feet five inches tall, maybe 120 pounds. But she'd spent years hiking through these mountains and working hard.

Ms. Menard explained. Forty years

ago she'd married one of the grandsons of the murdered Oscar Cosgrove. She had shared his poverty. Then, when her husband had died young, she'd married Claude Menard and returned here to open the curio shop.

"They—the greedy offspring of Amos Cosgrove—took everything that Oscar's children deserved," Ms. Menard went on. "But I had one small thing left. Mr. Peebles sold me ten acres for the curio shop. That was all I had to help my son, and for my own old age. Then Mrs. Chance hired the lawyers, and they told us we didn't have a right to this land! Even that—the last thing—they would have taken from us!" Ms. Menard cried.

But at that point she stopped her story abruptly. She never admitted that she had been behind the howling or the rapping sounds. She said nothing about the bloody rag, the cow's skull, or the many other harassments of Chalet 17. But Nina knew. At last, she *knew*—so she sped back to Mr. Cowles' office. She was surprised that Mrs. Chance was still there, ranting on and on.

Bursting into the office, Nina said, "Mrs. Chance, I have bad news for you. You can't evict Mr. Peebles and Ms. Menard. They must keep their land."

"Is that so? And just *why*, might I ask?" Mrs. Chance demanded.

"Picture this, Mrs. Chance," Nina said in an impassioned voice. "Picture a series of stories on TV about the old Cosgrove murders—how a young man killed his brother and got away with it. The public just *loves* sensational, gory stories. The reporters would be happy to explain how the dead boy's son was shunned and disinherited. And how all the offspring of the victim were cheated, generation after generation. And now— how a nice old man is losing his land, and an innocent little widow lady is losing her curio shop. And all because the greedy family of the murderer isn't satisfied. No, they still want more. . . ."

Mrs. Chance's face turned ashen. "You *wouldn't*! Those horrid media hounds would destroy us!"

"Yes, I'm afraid they would," Mr. Cowles nervously agreed as he protectively put his hand on her arm. "What will we do? This is so unfair, my dear Mrs. Chance!"

"We'll leave the old woman's junk shop alone, you idiot!" Mrs. Chance cried. "And we'll have to let the old man keep his land. We couldn't bear the bad publicity. We'll have to expand down the *other* side of the mountain!"

Nina stared at her coldly. Her heart was beating fast. "That would be a wise move, Mrs. Chance. Because if you don't—I'll help Mr. Peebles and Ms. Menard ruin you. I promise you that cow skulls landing on beds will be the *least* of your worries!" Nina Blake snapped. Mrs. Chance was stunned. She could only gasp as Nina walked out, slamming the door behind her.

"What happened in there?" Brian asked, catching up to Nina.

"I just quit," she said. "I'm packing my stuff and heading off the mountain."

Brian grabbed Nina and kissed her. Then he said, "Wait a minute for me. I'll be right behind you!"

COMPREHENSION QUESTIONS

RECALL

1. What unusual task did Mr. Cowles assign to Nina?

2. What frightening object did Nina find in the snow outside Chalet 17?

3. Who did Leo Peebles think was causing the strange events at Chalet 17?

IDENTIFYING CHARACTERS

1. Who owned the High Chalets Resort?

2. Who left flowers at Oscar Cosgrove's grave?

3. Who owned the curio shop near Leo Peebles' house?

VOCABULARY

1. What do the letters *SUV* stand for?

2. If High Chalets lost too much money, Nina was afraid that Mrs. Chance might "raze" the whole place. What does *raze* mean?

3. It made Nina sick to see Mr. Cowles "fawning" over Mrs. Chance. What does *fawning* mean?

DRAWING CONCLUSIONS

1. What conclusion did Nina finally draw about who was harassing Chalet 17?

2. When they first set eyes on the caretaker of the cemetery, what conclusion did Nina and Brian draw?